31901066638745

CONTRA COSTA COUNTY LIBRARY

P9-AFL-914

You Are a WRITER!

April Jones Prince

Illustrated by
Christine Davenier

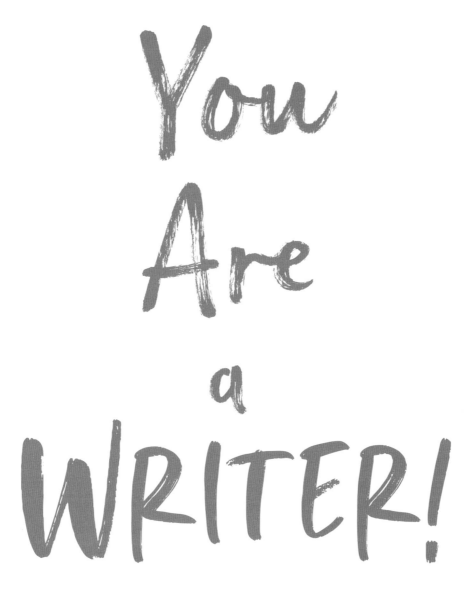

MARGARET FERGUSON BOOKS
HOLIDAY HOUSE · NEW YORK

Margaret Ferguson Books

Text copyright © 2021 by April Jones Prince

Illustrations copyright © 2021 by Christine Davenier

All Rights Reserved

HOLIDAY HOUSE is registered in the U.S. Patent and Trademark Office.

Printed and bound in April 2021 at C&C Offset, Shenzhen, China.

The artwork was created with Moleskine paper and ink (Ecoline and Colorex).

www.holidayhouse.com

First Edition

1 3 5 7 9 10 8 6 4 2

Library of Congress Cataloging-in-Publication Data

Names: Prince, April Jones, author. | Davenier, Christine, illustrator.

Title: You are a reader! ; You are a writer! / by April Jones Prince ; illustrated by Christine Davenier.

Other titles: You are a writer!

Description: First edition. | New York : Holiday House, 2021. | Titles from

separate title pages; works issued back-to-back and inverted

(tête-bêche format). | Audience: Ages 6 to 8. | Audience: Grades 2–3.

Summary: Illustrations and rhyming text celebrate readers

and writers and the way the two are intertwined.

Identifiers: LCCN 2020018800 | ISBN 9780823446254 (hardcover)

Subjects: LCSH: Upside-down books—Specimens. | CYAC: Stories in rhyme.

Books and reading—Fiction. | Authorship—Fiction. | Upside-down books.

Classification: LCC PZ8.3.P93 Yo 2021 | DDC [E]—dc23

LC record available at https://lccn.loc.gov/2020018800

ISBN: 978-0-8234-4625-4 (hardcover)

Wake, watch,

wonder, plot.

You can weave with words and thoughts.

Tell your story,

make your mark.

You can help ideas spark!

You have passion,

you have zest.

Use them on your writing quest.

Look around and listen well.
It's your job to touch-taste-smell.

Classroom,

kitchen,

park,

or fair.

You're a writer everywhere.

Still staring at an empty page?

Every writer knows that stage.

Ask "What if?"

Change your view.

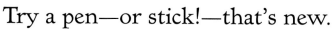

Try a pen—or stick!—that's new.

You might stumble,

you might sigh.

But writers read,

and draft,

and FLY!
(Don't give up!
You're doing fine!)

Try juicy words—they're more than "nice."
Juicy words have spunk and spice!

gooey STICKY

PLUMP

STELLAR tumble

crackle flutter

soar

GIGANTIC

Use details too, the super-tool
that boosts your words like rocket fuel
to let you "show" instead of "tell"
and cast your magic writer's spell.

And if your story won't ignite,
choose another thing to write.

Jot a journal,

sing your song.

Try a slogan, short and strong.

USE
YOUR VOICE
VOTE!

Pen a poem,

type a text.

Write a "thank you" at your desk.

And when the wordstream starts to flow,

get it down, now, swift or slow!

Cut and paste and edit later.

You're the boss—you're the creator.

Scribe by night . . .

or draft by day.

You have mighty things to say.

Hear the stories in your head,
bake them into epic bread.
Write to share your hopes and notions
or to sort out tough emotions.

SONG ★ ★
wish fairy

Tallest tales, or stories true—
they are gifts designed by YOU.
So think 'em up, write 'em down.
'Cause you are a . . .

castle KNIGHT

WRITER!

And writers are readers and readers are writers

and readers are writers . . .

and writers are readers . . .

And readers are writers and writers are readers

READER!

Find the facts, learn the truth.
You're an information sleuth.
Tallest tales or stories true—
they're an author's gift to you.
So soak them up, drink them down.
Cause you are a . . .

Reading is like milk and bread—

feeds your thirsty, hungry head.

You can dream! Imagine! Muse!

Slip on someone else's shoes.

Their worlds feel rich and real;
their actions make you gasp or squeal.

Favorite stories steal your heart
with characters who stand apart:

They're brave!

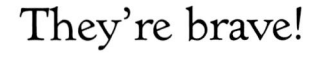

And strong!

With clever wit,

style, pluck, or downright grit.

Gather 'round on rug or chair.

Share a story anywhere!

The Magic Tree

There's cozy reading on your bed

or inside a fort instead.

A recipe that you can cook.

Magazines!

Maps, directions.
Menus full of sweet selections.

Storybooks aren't quite your speed?
So many other things to read!

Labels,

programs,

comic books.

Search until you find the thing
that makes your reading radar ping!

And when a story makes you grin,
clap and cheer and shriek, "Again!"

and FLY!
(Don't give up!
It's worth your while!)

grow,

But readers practice,

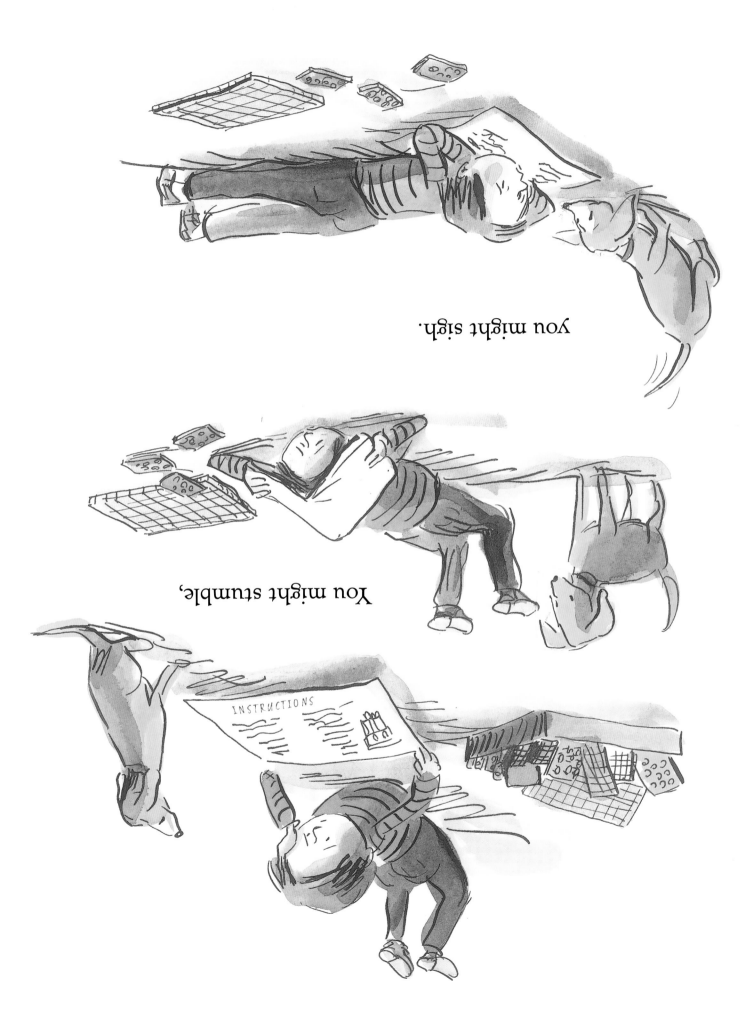

You might stumble,

You might sigh.

Stretch that word!
Sound it out.

Give your letter sounds a scout.

Spy a word that makes you scowl?
Trips you up with tricky vowels?

You might borrow.

You might shop.

You can even read and swap.

Do you open?

Swipe and tap?

Maybe listen in a lap?

Scan, sound,

simmer, think.

You can guzzle words and ink!

For my exceptional mom, my very first reader, whose energy,
creativity, and pluck inspire me every day—and who saved all
my childhood writing in a ginormous, juicy scrapbook.

Oodles of thanks to Lauren, phenomenal friend and teacher,
and to her fellow educators who help foster a love of reading
and writing in their students.
—A.J.P.

For my dear mother, who was a wonderful teacher and taught
me how to read and how to write.
—C.D.

A portion of the author's proceeds supports reading and writing programs for young
people, including First Book and the 826 National network of youth writing centers.

You Are a READER!

WITHDRAWN

April Jones Prince

Illustrated by
Christine Davenier

MARGARET FERGUSON BOOKS
HOLIDAY HOUSE · NEW YORK